DON QU

by Miguel de Cervantes

Translated by John Ormsby

Volume I., Part 12

CHAPTER XXX.

WHICH TREATS OF ADDRESS DISPLAYED BY THE FAIR DOROTHEA, WITH OTHER MATTERS PLEASANT AND AMUSING

The curate had hardly ceased speaking, when Sancho said, "In faith, then, senor licentiate, he who did that deed was my master; and it was not for want of my telling him beforehand and warning him to mind what he was about, and that it was a sin to set them at liberty, as they were all on the march there because they were special scoundrels."

"Blockhead!" said Don Quixote at this, "it is no business or concern of knights-errant to inquire whether any persons in affliction, in chains, or oppressed that they may meet on the high roads go that way and suffer as they do because of their faults or because of their misfortunes. It only concerns them to aid them as persons in need of help, having regard to their sufferings and not to their rascalities. I encountered a chaplet or string of miserable and unfortunate people, and did for them what my sense of duty demands of me, and as for the rest be that as it may; and whoever takes objection to it, saving the sacred dignity of the senor licentiate and his honoured person, I say he knows little about chivalry and lies like a whoreson villain, and this I will give him to know to the fullest extent with my sword;" and so saying he settled himself in his stirrups and pressed down his morion; for the barber's basin, which according to him was Mambrino's helmet, he carried hanging at the saddle-bow until he could repair the damage done to it by the galley slaves.

Dorothea, who was shrewd and sprightly, and by this time thoroughly understood Don Quixote's crazy turn, and that all except Sancho Panza were making game of him, not to be behind the rest said to him, on observing his irritation, "Sir Knight, remember the boon you have promised me, and that in accordance with it you must not engage in any other adventure, be it ever so pressing; calm yourself, for if the licentiate had known that the galley slaves had been set free by that unconquered arm he would have stopped his mouth thrice over, or even bitten his tongue three times before he would have said a word that tended towards disrespect of your worship."

"That I swear heartily," said the curate, "and I would have even plucked off a moustache."

"I will hold my peace, senora," said Don Quixote, "and I will curb the natural anger that had arisen in my breast, and will proceed in peace and quietness until I have fulfilled my promise; but in return for this consideration I entreat you to tell me, if you have no objection to do so, what is the nature of your trouble, and how many, who, and what are the persons of whom I am to require due satisfaction, and on whom I am to take vengeance on your behalf?"

"That I will do with all my heart," replied Dorothea, "if it will not be wearisome to you to hear of miseries and misfortunes."

"It will not be wearisome, senora," said Don Quixote; to which Dorothea replied, "Well, if that be so, give me your attention." As soon as she said this, Cardenio and the barber drew close to her side, eager to hear what sort of story the quick-witted Dorothea would invent for herself; and Sancho did the same, for he was as much taken in by her as his master; and she having settled herself comfortably in the saddle, and with the help of coughing and other preliminaries taken time to think, began with great sprightliness of manner in this fashion.

"First of all, I would have you know, sirs, that my name is-" and here she stopped for a moment, for she forgot the name the curate had given her; but he came to her relief, seeing what her difficulty was, and said, "It is no wonder, senora, that your highness should be confused and embarrassed in telling the tale of your misfortunes; for such afflictions often have the effect of depriving the sufferers of memory, so that they do not even remember their own names, as is the case now with your ladyship, who has forgotten that she is called the Princess Micomicona, lawful heiress of the great kingdom of Micomicon; and with this cue your highness may now recall to your sorrowful recollection all you may wish to tell us."

"That is the truth," said the damsel; "but I think from this on I shall have no need of any prompting, and I shall bring my true story safe into port, and here it is. The king my father, who was called Tinacrio the Sapient, was very learned in what they call magic arts, and became aware by his craft that my mother, who was called Queen Jaramilla, was to die before he did, and that soon after he too was to depart this life, and I was to be left an orphan without father or mother. But all this, he declared, did not so much grieve or distress him as his certain knowledge that a prodigious giant, the lord of a great island close to our kingdom, Pandafilando of the Scowl by name--for it is averred that, though his eyes are properly placed and straight, he always looks askew as if he squinted, and this he does out of malignity, to strike fear and terror into those he looks at--that he knew, I say, that this giant on becoming aware of my orphan condition would overrun my kingdom with a mighty force and strip me of all, not leaving me even a small village to shelter me; but that I could avoid all this ruin and misfortune if I were willing to marry him; however, as far as he could see, he never expected that I would consent to a marriage so unequal; and he said no more than the truth in this, for it has never entered my mind to marry that giant, or any other, let him be ever so great or enormous. My father said, too, that when he was dead, and I saw Pandafilando about to invade my kingdom, I was not to wait and attempt to defend myself, for that would be destructive to me, but that I should leave the kingdom entirely open to him if I wished to avoid the death and total destruction of my good and loyal vassals, for there would be no possibility of defending myself against the giant's devilish power; and that I should at once with some of my followers set out for Spain, where I should obtain relief in my distress on finding a certain knight-errant whose fame by that time would extend over the whole kingdom, and who would be called, if I remember rightly, Don Azote or Don Gigote."

"'Don Quixote,' he must have said, senora," observed Sancho at this, "otherwise called the Knight of the Rueful Countenance."

"That is it," said Dorothea; "he said, moreover, that he would be tall of stature and lank featured; and that on his right side under the left shoulder, or thereabouts, he would have a grey mole with hairs like bristles."

On hearing this, Don Quixote said to his squire, "Here, Sancho my son, bear a hand and help me to strip, for I want to see if I am the knight that sage king foretold."

"What does your worship want to strip for?" said Dorothea.

"To see if I have that mole your father spoke of," answered Don Quixote.

"There is no occasion to strip," said Sancho; "for I know your worship has just such a mole on the middle of your backbone, which is the mark of a strong man."

"That is enough," said Dorothea, "for with friends we must not look too closely into trifles; and whether it be on the shoulder or on the backbone matters little; it is enough if there is a mole, be it where it may, for it is all the same flesh; no doubt my good father hit the truth in every particular, and I have made a lucky hit in commending myself to Don Quixote; for he is the one my father spoke of, as the features of his countenance correspond with those assigned to this knight by that wide fame he has acquired not only in Spain but in all La Mancha; for I had scarcely landed at Osuna when I heard such accounts of his achievements, that at once my heart told me he was the very one I had come in search of."

"But how did you land at Osuna, senora," asked Don Quixote, "when it is not a seaport?"

But before Dorothea could reply the curate anticipated her, saying, "The princess meant to say that after she had landed at Malaga the first place where she heard of your worship was Osuna."

"That is what I meant to say," said Dorothea.

"And that would be only natural," said the curate. "Will your majesty please proceed?"

"There is no more to add," said Dorothea, "save that in finding Don Quixote I have had such good fortune, that I already reckon and regard myself queen and mistress of my entire dominions, since of his courtesy and magnanimity he has granted me the boon of accompanying me whithersoever I may conduct him, which will be only to bring him face to face with Pandafilando of the Scowl, that he may slay him and restore to me what has been unjustly usurped by him: for all this must come to pass satisfactorily since my good father Tinacrio the Sapient foretold it, who likewise left it declared in writing in Chaldee or Greek characters (for I cannot read them), that if this predicted knight, after having cut the giant's throat, should be disposed to marry me I was to offer myself at once without demur as his lawful wife, and yield him possession of my kingdom together with my person."

"What thinkest thou now, friend Sancho?" said Don Quixote at this. "Hearest thou that? Did I not tell thee so? See how we have already got a kingdom to govern and a queen to marry!"

"On my oath it is so," said Sancho; "and foul fortune to him who won't marry after slitting Senor Pandahilado's windpipe! And then, how illfavoured the queen is! I wish the fleas in my bed were that sort!"

And so saying he cut a couple of capers in the air with every sign of extreme satisfaction, and then ran to seize the bridle of Dorothea's mule, and checking it fell on his knees before her, begging her to give him her hand to kiss in token of his acknowledgment of her as his queen and mistress. Which of the bystanders could have helped laughing to see the madness of the master and the simplicity of the servant? Dorothea therefore gave her hand, and promised to make him a great lord in her kingdom, when Heaven should be so good as to permit her to recover and enjoy it, for which Sancho returned thanks in words that set them all laughing again.

"This, sirs," continued Dorothea, "is my story; it only remains to tell you that of all the attendants I took with me from my kingdom I have none left except this well-bearded squire, for all were drowned in a great tempest we encountered when in sight of port; and he and I came to land on a couple of planks as if by a miracle; and indeed the whole course of my life is a miracle and a mystery as you may have observed; and if I have been over minute in any respect or not as precise as I ought, let it be

4

accounted for by what the licentiate said at the beginning of my tale, that constant and excessive troubles deprive the sufferers of their memory."

"They shall not deprive me of mine, exalted and worthy princess," said Don Quixote, "however great and unexampled those which I shall endure in your service may be; and here I confirm anew the boon I have promised you, and I swear to go with you to the end of the world until I find myself in the presence of your fierce enemy, whose haughty head I trust by the aid of my arm to cut off with the edge of this--I will not say good sword, thanks to Gines de Pasamonte who carried away mine"--(this he said between his teeth, and then continued), "and when it has been cut off and you have been put in peaceful possession of your realm it shall be left to your own decision to dispose of your person as may be most pleasing to you; for so long as my memory is occupied, my will enslaved, and my understanding enthralled by her--I say no more--it is impossible for me for a moment to contemplate marriage, even with a Phoenix."

The last words of his master about not wanting to marry were so disagreeable to Sancho that raising his voice he exclaimed with great irritation:

"By my oath, Senor Don Quixote, you are not in your right senses; for how can your worship possibly object to marrying such an exalted princess as this? Do you think Fortune will offer you behind every stone such a piece of luck as is offered you now? Is my lady Dulcinea fairer, perchance? Not she; nor half as fair; and I will even go so far as to say she does not come up to the shoe of this one here. A poor chance I have of getting that county I am waiting for if your worship goes looking for dainties in the bottom of the sea. In the devil's name, marry, marry, and take this kingdom that comes to hand without any trouble, and when you are king make me a marquis or governor of a province, and for the rest let the devil take it all."

Don Quixote, when he heard such blasphemies uttered against his lady Dulcinea, could not endure it, and lifting his pike, without saying anything to Sancho or uttering a word, he gave him two such thwacks that he brought him to the ground; and had it not been that Dorothea cried out to him to spare him he would have no doubt taken his life on the spot.

"Do you think," he said to him after a pause, "you scurvy clown, that you are to be always interfering with me, and that you are to be always offending and I always pardoning? Don't fancy it, impious scoundrel, for that beyond a doubt thou art, since thou hast set thy tongue going against the peerless Dulcinea. Know you not, lout, vagabond, beggar, that were it not for the might that she infuses into my arm I should not have strength enough to kill a flea? Say, scoffer with a viper's tongue, what think you has won this kingdom and cut off this giant's head and made you a marquis (for all this I count as already accomplished and decided), but the might of Dulcinea, employing my arm as the instrument of her achievements? She fights in me and conquers in me, and I live and breathe in her, and owe my life and being to her. O whoreson scoundrel, how ungrateful you are, you see yourself raised from the dust of the earth to be a titled lord, and the return you make for so great a benefit is to speak evil of her who has conferred it upon you!"

Sancho was not so stunned but that he heard all his master said, and rising with some degree of nimbleness he ran to place himself behind Dorothea's palfrey, and from that position he said to his master:

"Tell me, senor; if your worship is resolved not to marry this great princess, it is plain the kingdom will not be yours; and not being so, how can you bestow favours upon me? That is what I complain of. Let your worship at any rate marry this queen, now that we have got her here as if showered down from heaven, and afterwards you may go back to my lady Dulcinea; for there must have been kings in the world who kept mistresses. As to beauty, I have nothing to do with it; and if the truth is to be told, I like them both; though I have never seen the lady Dulcinea."

"How! never seen her, blasphemous traitor!" exclaimed Don Quixote; "hast thou not just now brought me a message from her?"

"I mean," said Sancho, "that I did not see her so much at my leisure that I could take particular notice of her beauty, or of her charms piecemeal; but taken in the lump I like her."

"Now I forgive thee," said Don Quixote; "and do thou forgive me the injury I have done thee; for our first impulses are not in our control."

"That I see," replied Sancho, "and with me the wish to speak is always the first impulse, and I cannot help saying, once at any rate, what I have on the tip of my tongue."

"For all that, Sancho," said Don Quixote, "take heed of what thou sayest, for the pitcher goes so often to the well--I need say no more to thee."

"Well, well," said Sancho, "God is in heaven, and sees all tricks, and will judge who does most harm, I in not speaking right, or your worship in not doing it."

"That is enough," said Dorothea; "run, Sancho, and kiss your lord's hand and beg his pardon, and henceforward be more circumspect with your praise and abuse; and say nothing in disparagement of that lady Toboso, of whom I know nothing save that I am her servant; and put your trust in God, for you will not fail to obtain some dignity so as to live like a prince."

Sancho advanced hanging his head and begged his master's hand, which Don Quixote with dignity presented to him, giving him his blessing as soon as he had kissed it; he then bade him go on ahead a little, as he had questions to ask him and matters of great importance to discuss with him. Sancho obeyed, and when the two had gone some distance in advance Don Quixote said to him, "Since thy return I have had no opportunity or time to ask thee many particulars touching thy mission and the answer thou hast brought back, and now that chance has granted us the time and opportunity, deny me not the happiness thou canst give me by such good news."

"Let your worship ask what you will," answered Sancho, "for I shall find a way out of all as as I found a way in; but I implore you, senor, not not to be so revengeful in future."

"Why dost thou say that, Sancho?" said Don Quixote.

"I say it," he returned, "because those blows just now were more because of the quarrel the devil stirred up between us both the other night, than for what I said against my lady Dulcinea, whom I love and reverence as I would a relic--though there is nothing of that about her--merely as something belonging to your worship."

"Say no more on that subject for thy life, Sancho," said Don Quixote, "for it is displeasing to me; I have already pardoned thee for that, and thou knowest the common saying, 'for a fresh sin a fresh penance.'"

While this was going on they saw coming along the road they were following a man mounted on an ass, who when he came close seemed to be a gipsy; but Sancho Panza, whose eyes and heart were there wherever he saw asses, no sooner beheld the man than he knew him to be Gines de Pasamonte; and by the thread of the gipsy he got at the ball, his ass, for it was, in fact, Dapple that carried Pasamonte, who to escape recognition and to sell the ass had disguised himself as a gipsy, being able to speak the gipsy language, and many more, as well as if they were his own. Sancho saw him and recognised him, and the instant he did so he shouted to him, "Ginesillo, you thief, give up my treasure, release my life, embarrass thyself not with my repose, quit my ass, leave my delight, be off, rip, get thee gone, thief, and give up what is not thine."

There was no necessity for so many words or objurgations, for at the first one Gines jumped down, and at a like racing speed made off and got clear of them all. Sancho hastened to his Dapple, and embracing him he said, "How hast thou fared, my blessing, Dapple of my eyes, my comrade?" all the while kissing him and caressing him as if he were a human being. The ass held his peace, and let himself be kissed and caressed by Sancho without answering a single word. They all came up and congratulated him on having found Dapple, Don Quixote especially, who told him that notwithstanding this he would not cancel the order for the three ass-colts, for which Sancho thanked him.

While the two had been going along conversing in this fashion, the curate observed to Dorothea that she had shown great cleverness, as well in the story itself as in its conciseness, and the resemblance it bore to those of the books of chivalry. She said that she had many times amused herself reading them; but that she did not know the situation of the provinces or seaports, and so she had said at haphazard that she had landed at Osuna.

"So I saw," said the curate, "and for that reason I made haste to say what I did, by which it was all set right. But is it not a strange thing to see how readily this unhappy gentleman believes all these figments and lies, simply because they are in the style and manner of the absurdities of his books?"

"So it is," said Cardenio; "and so uncommon and unexampled, that were one to attempt to invent and concoct it in fiction, I doubt if there be any wit keen enough to imagine it."

"But another strange thing about it," said the curate, "is that, apart from the silly things which this worthy gentleman says in connection with his craze, when other subjects are dealt with, he can discuss them in a perfectly rational manner, showing that his mind is quite clear and composed; so that, provided his chivalry is not touched upon, no one would take him to be anything but a man of thoroughly sound understanding."

While they were holding this conversation Don Quixote continued his with Sancho, saying:

"Friend Panza, let us forgive and forget as to our quarrels, and tell me now, dismissing anger and irritation, where, how, and when didst thou find Dulcinea? What was she doing? What didst thou say to her? What did she answer? How did she look when she was reading my letter? Who copied it out for thee? and everything in the matter that seems to thee worth knowing, asking, and learning; neither adding nor falsifying to give me pleasure, nor yet curtailing lest you should deprive me of it."

"Senor," replied Sancho, "if the truth is to be told, nobody copied out the letter for me, for I carried no letter at all."

"It is as thou sayest," said Don Quixote, "for the note-book in which I wrote it I found in my own possession two days after thy departure, which gave me very great vexation, as I knew not what thou wouldst do on finding thyself without any letter; and I made sure thou wouldst return from the place where thou didst first miss it."

"So I should have done," said Sancho, "if I had not got it by heart when your worship read it to me, so that I repeated it to a sacristan, who copied it out for me from hearing it, so exactly that he said in all the days of his life, though he had read many a letter of excommunication, he had never seen or read so pretty a letter as that."

"And hast thou got it still in thy memory, Sancho?" said Don Quixote.

"No, senor," replied Sancho, "for as soon as I had repeated it, seeing there was no further use for it, I set about forgetting it; and if I recollect any of it, it is that about 'Scrubbing,' I mean to say 'Sovereign Lady,' and the end 'Yours till death, the Knight of the Rueful Countenance;' and between these two I put into it more than three hundred 'my souls' and 'my life's' and 'my eyes."

CHAPTER XXXI.

OF THE DELECTABLE DISCUSSION BETWEEN DON QUIXOTE AND SANCHO PANZA, HIS SQUIRE, TOGETHER WITH OTHER INCIDENTS

"All that is not unsatisfactory to me," said Don Quixote. "Go on; thou didst reach her; and what was that queen of beauty doing? Surely thou didst find her stringing pearls, or embroidering some device in gold thread for this her enslaved knight."

"I did not," said Sancho, "but I found her winnowing two bushels of wheat in the yard of her house."

"Then depend upon it," said Don Quixote, "the grains of that wheat were pearls when touched by her hands; and didst thou look, friend? was it white wheat or brown?"

"It was neither, but red," said Sancho.

"Then I promise thee," said Don Quixote, "that, winnowed by her hands, beyond a doubt the bread it made was of the whitest; but go on;

when thou gavest her my letter, did she kiss it? Did she place it on her head? Did she perform any ceremony befitting it, or what did she do?"

"When I went to give it to her," replied Sancho, "she was hard at it swaying from side to side with a lot of wheat she had in the sieve, and she said to me, 'Lay the letter, friend, on the top of that sack, for I cannot read it until I have done sifting all this."

"Discreet lady!" said Don Quixote; "that was in order to read it at her leisure and enjoy it; proceed, Sancho; while she was engaged in her occupation what converse did she hold with thee? What did she ask about me, and what answer didst thou give? Make haste; tell me all, and let not an atom be left behind in the ink-bottle."

"She asked me nothing," said Sancho; "but I told her how your worship was left doing penance in her service, naked from the waist up, in among these mountains like a savage, sleeping on the ground, not eating bread off a tablecloth nor combing your beard, weeping and cursing your fortune."

"In saying I cursed my fortune thou saidst wrong," said Don Quixote; "for rather do I bless it and shall bless it all the days of my life for having made me worthy of aspiring to love so lofty a lady as Dulcinea del Toboso."

"And so lofty she is," said Sancho, "that she overtops me by more than a hand's-breadth."

"What! Sancho," said Don Quixote, "didst thou measure with her?"

"I measured in this way," said Sancho; "going to help her to put a sack of wheat on the back of an ass, we came so close together that I could see she stood more than a good palm over me."

"Well!" said Don Quixote, "and doth she not of a truth accompany and adorn this greatness with a thousand million charms of mind! But one thing thou wilt not deny, Sancho; when thou camest close to her didst thou not perceive a Sabaean odour, an aromatic fragrance, a, I know not what, delicious, that I cannot find a name for; I mean a redolence, an exhalation, as if thou wert in the shop of some dainty glover?"

"All I can say is," said Sancho, "that I did perceive a little odour, something goaty; it must have been that she was all in a sweat with hard work."

"It could not be that," said Don Quixote, "but thou must have been suffering from cold in the head, or must have smelt thyself; for I know well what would be the scent of that rose among thorns, that lily of the field, that dissolved amber."

"Maybe so," replied Sancho; "there often comes from myself that same odour which then seemed to me to come from her grace the lady Dulcinea; but that's no wonder, for one devil is like another."

"Well then," continued Don Quixote, "now she has done sifting the corn and sent it to the mill; what did she do when she read the letter?"

"As for the letter," said Sancho, "she did not read it, for she said she could neither read nor write; instead of that she tore it up into small pieces, saying that she did not want to let anyone read it lest her secrets should become known in the village, and that what I had told her by word of mouth about the love your worship bore her, and the extraordinary penance you were doing for her sake, was enough; and, to make an end of it, she told me to tell your worship that she kissed your hands, and that she had a greater desire to see you than to write to you; and that therefore she entreated and commanded you, on sight of this present, to come out of these thickets, and to have done with carrying on absurdities, and to set out at once for El Toboso, unless something else of greater importance should happen, for she had a great desire to see your worship. She laughed greatly when I told her how your worship was called The Knight of the Rueful Countenance; I asked her if that Biscayan the other day had been there; and she told me he had, and that he was an honest fellow; I asked her too about the galley slaves, but she said she had not seen any as yet."

"So far all goes well," said Don Quixote; "but tell me what jewel was it that she gave thee on taking thy leave, in return for thy tidings of me? For it is a usual and ancient custom with knights and ladies errant to give the squires, damsels, or dwarfs who bring tidings of their ladies to the knights, or of their knights to the ladies, some rich jewel as a guerdon for good news,' and acknowledgment of the message."

"That is very likely," said Sancho, "and a good custom it was, to my mind; but that must have been in days gone by, for now it would seem to be the custom only to give a piece of bread and cheese; because that was what my lady Dulcinea gave me over the top of the yard-wall when I took leave of her; and more by token it was sheep's-milk cheese."

"She is generous in the extreme," said Don Quixote, "and if she did not give thee a jewel of gold, no doubt it must have been because she had not one to hand there to give thee; but sleeves are good after Easter; I shall see her and all shall be made right. But knowest thou what amazes me, Sancho? It seems to me thou must have gone and come through the air, for thou hast taken but little more than three days to go to El Toboso and return, though it is more than thirty leagues from here to there. From which I am inclined to think that the sage magician who is my friend, and watches over my interests (for of necessity there is and must be one, or else I should not be a right knight-errant), that this same, I say, must have helped thee to travel without thy knowledge; for some of these sages will catch up a knight-errant sleeping in his bed, and without his knowing how or in what way it happened, he wakes up the next day more than a thousand leagues away from the place where he went to sleep. And if it were not for this, knights-errant would not be able to give aid to one another in peril, as they do at every turn. For a knight, maybe, is fighting in the mountains of Armenia with some dragon, or fierce serpent, or another knight, and gets the worst of the battle, and is at the point of death; but when he least looks for it, there appears over against him on a cloud, or chariot of fire, another knight, a friend of his, who just before had been in England, and who takes his part, and delivers him from death; and at night he finds himself in his own quarters supping very much to his satisfaction; and yet from one place to the other will have been two or three thousand leagues. And all this is done by the craft and skill of the sage enchanters who take care of those valiant knights; so that, friend Sancho, I find no difficulty in believing that thou mayest have gone from this place to El Toboso and returned in such a short time, since, as I have said, some friendly sage must have carried thee through the air without thee perceiving it."

"That must have been it," said Sancho, "for indeed Rocinante went like a gipsy's ass with quicksilver in his ears."

"Quicksilver!" said Don Quixote, "aye and what is more, a legion of devils, folk that can travel and make others travel without being weary, exactly as the whim seizes them. But putting this aside, what thinkest thou I ought to do about my lady's command to go and see her? For though I feel that I am bound to obey her mandate, I feel too that I am debarred by the boon I have accorded to the princess that accompanies us, and the law of chivalry compels me to have regard for my word in preference to my inclination; on the one hand the desire to see my lady pursues and harasses me, on the other my solemn promise and the glory I shall win in this enterprise urge and call me; but what I think I shall do is to travel with all speed and reach quickly the place where this giant is, and on my arrival I shall cut off his head, and establish the princess peacefully in her realm, and forthwith I shall return to behold the light that lightens my senses, to whom I shall make such excuses that she will be led to approve of my delay, for she will see that it entirely tends to increase her glory and fame; for all that I have won, am winning, or shall win by arms in this life, comes to me of the favour she extends to me, and because I am hers."

"Ah! what a sad state your worship's brains are in!" said Sancho. "Tell me, senor, do you mean to travel all that way for nothing, and to let slip and lose so rich and great a match as this where they give as a portion a kingdom that in sober truth I have heard say is more than twenty thousand leagues round about, and abounds with all things necessary to support human life, and is bigger than Portugal and Castile put together? Peace, for the love of God! Blush for what you have said, and take my advice, and forgive me, and marry at once in the first village where there is a curate; if not, here is our licentiate who will do the business beautifully; remember, I am old enough to give advice, and this I am giving comes pat to the purpose; for a sparrow in the hand is better than a vulture on the wing, and he who has the good to his hand and chooses the bad, that the good he complains of may not come to him."

"Look here, Sancho," said Don Quixote. "If thou art advising me to marry, in order that immediately on slaying the giant I may become king, and be able to confer favours on thee, and give thee what I have promised, let me tell thee I shall be able very easily to satisfy thy desires without marrying; for before going into battle I will make it a stipulation that, if I come out of it victorious, even I do not marry, they shall give me a portion portion of the kingdom, that I may bestow it upon whomsoever I choose, and when they give it to me upon whom wouldst thou have me bestow it but upon thee?"

"That is plain speaking," said Sancho; "but let your worship take care to choose it on the seacoast, so that if I don't like the life, I may be able to ship off my black vassals and deal with them as I have said; don't mind going to see my lady Dulcinea now, but go and kill this giant and let us finish off this business; for by God it strikes me it will be one of great honour and great profit."

"I hold thou art in the right of it, Sancho," said Don Quixote, "and I will take thy advice as to accompanying the princess before going to see Dulcinea; but I counsel thee not to say anything to any one, or to those who are with us, about what we have considered and discussed, for as Dulcinea is so decorous that she does not wish her thoughts to be known it is not right that I or anyone for me should disclose them."

"Well then, if that be so," said Sancho, "how is it that your worship makes all those you overcome by your arm go to present themselves before my lady Dulcinea, this being the same thing as signing your name to it that you love her and are her lover? And as those who go must perforce kneel before her and say they come from your worship to submit themselves to her, how can the thoughts of both of you be hid?"

"O, how silly and simple thou art!" said Don Quixote; "seest thou not, Sancho, that this tends to her greater exaltation? For thou must know that according to our way of thinking in chivalry, it is a high honour to a lady to have many knights-errant in her service, whose thoughts never go beyond serving her for her own sake, and who look for no other reward for their great and true devotion than that she should be willing to accept them as her knights."

"It is with that kind of love," said Sancho, "I have heard preachers say we ought to love our Lord, for himself alone, without being moved by the hope of glory or the fear of punishment; though for my part, I would rather love and serve him for what he could do."

"The devil take thee for a clown!" said Don Quixote, "and what shrewd things thou sayest at times! One would think thou hadst studied."

"In faith, then, I cannot even read."

Master Nicholas here called out to them to wait a while, as they wanted to halt and drink at a little spring there was there. Don Quixote drew up, not a little to the satisfaction of Sancho, for he was by this time weary of telling so many lies, and in dread of his master catching him tripping, for though he knew that Dulcinea was a peasant girl of El Toboso, he had never seen her in all his life. Cardenio had now put on the clothes which Dorothea was wearing when they found her, and though they were not very good, they were far better than those he put off. They dismounted together by the side of the spring, and with what the curate had provided himself with at the inn they appeased, though not very well, the keen appetite they all of them brought with them.

While they were so employed there happened to come by a youth passing on his way, who stopping to examine the party at the spring, the next moment ran to Don Quixote and clasping him round the legs, began to weep freely, saying, "O, senor, do you not know me? Look at me well; I am that lad Andres that your worship released from the oak-tree where I was tied."

Don Quixote recognised him, and taking his hand he turned to those present and said: "That your worships may see how important it is to have knights-errant to redress the wrongs and injuries done by tyrannical and wicked men in this world, I may tell you that some days ago passing through a wood, I heard cries and piteous complaints as of a person in pain and distress; I immediately hastened, impelled by my bounden duty, to the quarter whence the plaintive accents seemed to me to proceed, and I found tied to an oak this lad who now stands before you, which in my heart I rejoice at, for his testimony will not permit me to depart from the truth in any particular. He was, I say, tied to an oak, naked from the waist up, and a clown, whom I afterwards found to be his master, was scarifying him by lashes with the reins of his mare. As soon as I saw him I asked the reason of so cruel a flagellation. The boor replied that he was flogging him because he was his servant and because of carelessness that proceeded rather from dishonesty than stupidity; on which this boy said, 'Senor, he flogs me only because I ask for my wages.' The master made I know not what speeches and explanations, which, though I listened to them, I did not accept. In short, I compelled the clown to unbind him, and to swear he would take him with him, and pay him real by real, and perfumed into the bargain. Is not all this true, Andres my son? Didst thou not mark with what authority I commanded him, and with what humility he promised to do all I enjoined, specified, and required of him? Answer without hesitation; tell these gentlemen what took place, that they may see that it is as great an advantage as I say to have knights-errant abroad."

"All that your worship has said is quite true," answered the lad; "but the end of the business turned out just the opposite of what your worship supposes."

"How! the opposite?" said Don Quixote; "did not the clown pay thee then?"

"Not only did he not pay me," replied the lad, "but as soon as your worship had passed out of the wood and we were alone, he tied me up again to the same oak and gave me a fresh flogging, that left me like a flayed Saint Bartholomew; and every stroke he gave me he followed up with some jest or gibe about having made a fool of your worship, and but for the pain I was suffering I should have laughed at the things he said. In short he left me in such a condition that I have been until now in a hospital getting cured of the injuries which that rascally clown inflicted on me then; for all which your worship is to blame; for if you had gone your own way and not come where there was no call for you, nor meddled in other people's affairs, my master would have been content with giving me one or two dozen lashes, and would have then loosed me and paid me what he owed me; but when your worship abused him so out of measure, and gave him so many hard words, his anger was kindled; and as he could not revenge himself on you, as soon as he saw you had left him the storm burst upon me in such a way, that I feel as if I should never be a man again."

"The mischief," said Don Quixote, "lay in my going away; for I should not have gone until I had seen thee paid; because I ought to have known well by long experience that there is no clown who will keep his word if he finds it will not suit him to keep it; but thou rememberest, Andres, that I swore if he did not pay thee I would go and seek him, and find him though he were to hide himself in the whale's belly."

"That is true," said Andres; "but it was of no use."

"Thou shalt see now whether it is of use or not," said Don Quixote; and so saying, he got up hastily and bade Sancho bridle Rocinante, who was browsing while they were eating. Dorothea asked him what he meant to do. He replied that he meant to go in search of this clown and chastise him for such iniquitous conduct, and see Andres paid to the last maravedi, despite and in the teeth of all the clowns in the world. To which she replied that he must remember that in accordance with his promise he could not engage in any enterprise until he had concluded hers; and that as he knew this better than anyone, he should restrain his ardour until his return from her kingdom.

"That is true," said Don Quixote, "and Andres must have patience until my return as you say, senora; but I once more swear and promise not to stop until I have seen him avenged and paid."

"I have no faith in those oaths," said Andres; "I would rather have now something to help me to get to Seville than all the revenges in the

15

world; if you have here anything to eat that I can take with me, give it me, and God be with your worship and all knights-errant; and may their errands turn out as well for themselves as they have for me."

Sancho took out from his store a piece of bread and another of cheese, and giving them to the lad he said, "Here, take this, brother Andres, for we have all of us a share in your misfortune."

"Why, what share have you got?"

"This share of bread and cheese I am giving you," answered Sancho; "and God knows whether I shall feel the want of it myself or not; for I would have you know, friend, that we squires to knights-errant have to bear a great deal of hunger and hard fortune, and even other things more easily felt than told."

Andres seized his bread and cheese, and seeing that nobody gave him anything more, bent his head, and took hold of the road, as the saying is. However, before leaving he said, "For the love of God, sir knight-errant, if you ever meet me again, though you may see them cutting me to pieces, give me no aid or succour, but leave me to my misfortune, which will not be so great but that a greater will come to me by being helped by your worship, on whom and all the knights-errant that have ever been born God send his curse."

Don Quixote was getting up to chastise him, but he took to his heels at such a pace that no one attempted to follow him; and mightily chapfallen was Don Quixote at Andres' story, and the others had to take great care to restrain their laughter so as not to put him entirely out of countenance.

CHAPTER XXXII.

WHICH TREATS OF WHAT BEFELL DON QUIXOTE'S PARTY AT THE INN

Their dainty repast being finished, they saddled at once, and without any adventure worth mentioning they reached next day the inn, the object of Sancho Panza's fear and dread; but though he would have rather not entered it, there was no help for it. The landlady, the landlord, their daughter, and Maritornes, when they saw Don Quixote and Sancho coming, went out to welcome them with signs of hearty satisfaction, which Don Quixote received with dignity and gravity, and bade them make up a better bed for him than the last time: to which the landlady replied that if he paid better than he did the last time she would give him one fit for a prince. Don Quixote said he would, so they made up a tolerable one for him in the same garret as before; and he lay down at once, being sorely shaken and in want of sleep.

No sooner was the door shut upon him than the landlady made at the barber, and seizing him by the beard, said:

"By my faith you are not going to make a beard of my tail any longer; you must give me back tail, for it is a shame the way that thing of my husband's goes tossing about on the floor; I mean the comb that I used to stick in my good tail."

But for all she tugged at it the barber would not give it up until the licentiate told him to let her have it, as there was now no further occasion for that stratagem, because he might declare himself and appear in his own character, and tell Don Quixote that he had fled to this inn when those thieves the galley slaves robbed him; and should he ask for the princess's squire, they could tell him that she had sent him on before her to give notice to the people of her kingdom that she was coming, and bringing with her the deliverer of them all. On this the barber cheerfully restored the tail to the landlady, and at the same time they returned all the accessories they had borrowed to effect Don Quixote's deliverance. All the people of the inn were struck with astonishment at the beauty of Dorothea, and even at the comely figure of the shepherd Cardenio. The curate made them get ready such fare as there was in the inn, and the landlord, in hope of better payment, served them up a tolerably good dinner. All this time Don Quixote was asleep, and they thought it best not to waken him, as sleeping would now do him more good than eating.

While at dinner, the company consisting of the landlord, his wife, their daughter, Maritornes, and all the travellers, they discussed the strange craze of Don Quixote and the manner in which he had been found; and the landlady told them what had taken place between him and the carrier; and then, looking round to see if Sancho was there, when she saw he was not, she gave them the whole story of his blanketing, which they received with no little amusement. But on the curate observing that it was the books of chivalry which Don Quixote had read that had turned his brain, the landlord said:

"I cannot understand how that can be, for in truth to my mind there is no better reading in the world, and I have here two or three of them, with other writings that are the very life, not only of myself but of plenty more; for when it is harvest-time, the reapers flock here on holidays, and there is always one among them who can read and who takes up one of these books, and we gather round him, thirty or more of us, and stay listening to him with a delight that makes our grey hairs grow young again. At least I can say for myself that when I hear of what furious and terrible blows the knights deliver, I am seized with the longing to do the same, and I would like to be hearing about them night and day."

"And I just as much," said the landlady, "because I never have a quiet moment in my house except when you are listening to some one reading; for then you are so taken up that for the time being you forget to scold."

"That is true," said Maritornes; "and, faith, I relish hearing these things greatly too, for they are very pretty; especially when they describe some lady or another in the arms of her knight under the orange trees, and the duenna who is keeping watch for them half dead with envy and fright; all this I say is as good as honey."

"And you, what do you think, young lady?" said the curate turning to the landlord's daughter.

"I don't know indeed, senor," said she; "I listen too, and to tell the truth, though I do not understand it, I like hearing it; but it is not the blows that my father likes that I like, but the laments the knights utter when they are separated from their ladies; and indeed they sometimes make me weep with the pity I feel for them."

"Then you would console them if it was for you they wept, young lady?" said Dorothea.

"I don't know what I should do," said the girl; "I only know that there are some of those ladies so cruel that they call their knights tigers and lions and a thousand other foul names: and Jesus! I don't know what sort of folk they can be, so unfeeling and heartless, that rather than bestow a glance upon a worthy man they leave him to die or go mad. I don't know what is the good of such prudery; if it is for honour's sake, why not marry them? That's all they want."

"Hush, child," said the landlady; "it seems to me thou knowest a great deal about these things, and it is not fit for girls to know or talk so much."

"As the gentleman asked me, I could not help answering him," said the girl.

"Well then," said the curate, "bring me these books, senor landlord, for I should like to see them."

"With all my heart," said he, and going into his own room he brought out an old valise secured with a little chain, on opening which the curate found in it three large books and some manuscripts written in a very good hand. The first that he opened he found to be "Don Cirongilio of Thrace," and the second "Don Felixmarte of Hircania," and the other the "History of the Great Captain Gonzalo Hernandez de Cordova, with the Life of Diego Garcia de Paredes."

When the curate read the two first titles he looked over at the barber and said, "We want my friend's housekeeper and niece here now."

"Nay," said the barber, "I can do just as well to carry them to the yard or to the hearth, and there is a very good fire there."

"What! your worship would burn my books!" said the landlord.

"Only these two," said the curate, "Don Cirongilio, and Felixmarte."

"Are my books, then, heretics or phlegmaties that you want to burn them?" said the landlord.

"Schismatics you mean, friend," said the barber, "not phlegmatics."

"That's it," said the landlord; "but if you want to burn any, let it be that about the Great Captain and that Diego Garcia; for I would rather have a child of mine burnt than either of the others."

"Brother," said the curate, "those two books are made up of lies, and are full of folly and nonsense; but this of the Great Captain is a true history, and contains the deeds of Gonzalo Hernandez of Cordova, who by his many and great achievements earned the title all over the world of the Great Captain, a famous and illustrious name, and deserved by him alone; and this Diego Garcia de Paredes was a distinguished knight of the city of Trujillo in Estremadura, a most gallant soldier, and of such bodily strength that with one finger he stopped a mill-wheel in full motion; and posted with a two-handed sword at the foot of a bridge he kept the whole of an immense army from passing over it, and achieved such other exploits that if, instead of his relating them himself with the modesty of a knight and of one writing his own history, some free and unbiassed writer had recorded them, they would have thrown into the shade all the deeds of the Hectors, Achilleses, and Rolands."

"Tell that to my father," said the landlord. "There's a thing to be astonished at! Stopping a mill-wheel! By God your worship should read what I have read of Felixmarte of Hircania, how with one single backstroke he cleft five giants asunder through the middle as if they had been made of bean-pods like the little friars the children make; and another time he attacked a very great and powerful army, in which there were more than a million six hundred thousand soldiers, all armed from head to foot, and he routed them all as if they had been flocks of sheep."

"And then, what do you say to the good Cirongilio of Thrace, that was so stout and bold; as may be seen in the book, where it is related that as he was sailing along a river there came up out of the midst of the water against him a fiery serpent, and he, as soon as he saw it, flung himself upon it and got astride of its scaly shoulders, and squeezed its throat with both hands with such force that the serpent, finding he was throttling it, had nothing for it but to let itself sink to the bottom of the river, carrying with it the knight who would not let go his hold; and when they got down there he found himself among palaces and gardens so pretty that it was a wonder to see; and then the serpent changed itself into an old ancient man, who told him such things as were never heard. Hold your peace, senor; for if you were to hear this you would go mad with delight. A couple of figs for your Great Captain and your Diego Garcia!"

Hearing this Dorothea said in a whisper to Cardenio, "Our landlord is almost fit to play a second part to Don Quixote."

"I think so," said Cardenio, "for, as he shows, he accepts it as a certainty that everything those books relate took place exactly as it is

20

written down; and the barefooted friars themselves would not persuade him to the contrary."

"But consider, brother," said the curate once more, "there never was any Felixmarte of Hircania in the world, nor any Cirongilio of Thrace, or any of the other knights of the same sort, that the books of chivalry talk of; the whole thing is the fabrication and invention of idle wits, devised by them for the purpose you describe of beguiling the time, as your reapers do when they read; for I swear to you in all seriousness there never were any such knights in the world, and no such exploits or nonsense ever happened anywhere."

"Try that bone on another dog," said the landlord; "as if I did not know how many make five, and where my shoe pinches me; don't think to feed me with pap, for by God I am no fool. It is a good joke for your worship to try and persuade me that everything these good books say is nonsense and lies, and they printed by the license of the Lords of the Royal Council, as if they were people who would allow such a lot of lies to be printed all together, and so many battles and enchantments that they take away one's senses."

"I have told you, friend," said the curate, "that this is done to divert our idle thoughts; and as in well-ordered states games of chess, fives, and billiards are allowed for the diversion of those who do not care, or are not obliged, or are unable to work, so books of this kind are allowed to be printed, on the supposition that, what indeed is the truth, there can be nobody so ignorant as to take any of them for true stories; and if it were permitted me now, and the present company desired it, I could say something about the qualities books of chivalry should possess to be good ones, that would be to the advantage and even to the taste of some; but I hope the time will come when I can communicate my ideas to some one who may be able to mend matters; and in the meantime, senor landlord, believe what I have said, and take your books, and make up your mind about their truth or falsehood, and much good may they do you; and God grant you may not fall lame of the same foot your guest Don Quixote halts on."

"No fear of that," returned the landlord; "I shall not be so mad as to make a knight-errant of myself; for I see well enough that things are not now as they used to be in those days, when they say those famous knights roamed about the world."

Sancho had made his appearance in the middle of this conversation, and he was very much troubled and cast down by what he heard said about knights-errant being now no longer in vogue, and all books of chivalry being folly and lies; and he resolved in his heart to wait and see what came of this journey of his master's, and if it did not turn out as happily as his master expected, he determined to leave him and go back to his wife and children and his ordinary labour.

The landlord was carrying away the valise and the books, but the curate said to him, "Wait; I want to see what those papers are that are written in such a good hand." The landlord taking them out handed them to him to read, and he perceived they were a work of about eight sheets of manuscript, with, in large letters at the beginning, the title of "Novel of the Ill-advised Curiosity." The curate read three or four lines to himself, and said, "I must say the title of this novel does not seem to me a bad one, and I feel an inclination to read it all." To which the landlord replied, "Then your reverence will do well to read it, for I can tell you that some guests who have read it here have been much pleased with it, and have begged it of me very earnestly; but I would not give it, meaning to return it to the person who forgot the valise, books, and papers here, for maybe he will return here some time or other; and though I know I shall miss the books, faith I mean to return them; for though I am an innkeeper, still I am a Christian."

"You are very right, friend," said the curate; "but for all that, if the novel pleases me you must let me copy it."

"With all my heart," replied the host.

While they were talking Cardenio had taken up the novel and begun to read it, and forming the same opinion of it as the curate, he begged him to read it so that they might all hear it.

"I would read it," said the curate, "if the time would not be better spent in sleeping."

"It will be rest enough for me," said Dorothea, "to while away the time by listening to some tale, for my spirits are not yet tranquil enough to let me sleep when it would be seasonable."

"Well then, in that case," said the curate, "I will read it, if it were only out of curiosity; perhaps it may contain something pleasant."

Master Nicholas added his entreaties to the same effect, and Sancho too; seeing which, and considering that he would give pleasure to all, and receive it himself, the curate said, "Well then, attend to me everyone, for the novel begins thus."

Printed in Great Britain
by Amazon

25761795R00020